WOMEN ABOUT LOVE

INSIDE

OM SURAJ GUTTI

ISBN 979-888569730-9

I dedicate this book first to my parents who gave me all time freedom of choosing in each and every aspect. Later it was about my family and relatives who supported me in my entire life till now even i did wrong they corrected me. Next this is dedeciated to lot of my friends whom i'm being talking since a long time Lalitha Devi, Divya, Roshini, Yamini, Aleta, Dital, Kirti and all my friends.

Contents

Preface

"Women About Love" is not only a simple book with some set of words. It's compression of a thousands of peoples understanding, perspective, thinking, experinces and many with whom I spoke with and heard by. Initially i started talking with my friends, colleagues, business partners and others who all come in my life journey. At some point of time i realized there is a big misunderstanding aura is surrounded by everyone with their kind of thinking, situations facing etc. kinds. But all the thinking of misunderstanding coming by the wrong step of initial days where the relationship started. In every relationship the love is present or evolved but the evolution time every men goes into many circumstances to impress a women and also women also thinks many kind of situations of her life. This two are maximum intitally got matching but at the end of some day the understanding staying apart from each other that made many problems leading and effects many lifes in the society.

So i thought to write what i felt and what i know and what i observed on talking with a lot of lot of lot of women in my life. Every women has one perspective, thinking, situations, life etc. In this book I tried to wrote all of them in one set.

Prologue

L - Life

O - Of

V - Valuable

E - Emotion

This four words are driving many relationships into a starting a new life, some into crazy, some into end of chapters, some into wonders, etc.

1

Looking/Observing

She will not first see directly to any men; God give a power to them to know that who are seeing them and who are talking about them by a sense of attention which most of the men not have.

She will observe in a man first how he reacts first on the accordance of the situations which basically reveals the nature and character of a person.

She will next observe the person how he talks with others that shows his way of life style he grown up.

She will also see the person expenditure which shows his approach towards the value of money and also the respect towards it which reflects in the responsibility.

She lasts see about his way of dressing which many men think if he looks great then any girl will fall on him. that's false. that's not her first she thinks or see.

Even she not cares how he look truly she can change the things because they have belief on themselves.

In fact, they have ability to change.

Look

This we say in general terminology that "First Impression is Best Impression". This is the reason why still these days people will aware of looks and observing skills.

The looking of the person is not only by the dressing it also involves with hair style, beard, moustache, way of walking, body language and smile. Some people see the body fitness not some most of the women look that doesn't mean every one expect six pack body. atleast a good fitness to walk a certain distance.

2

First Approach

She will wait to observe how he will approach on his first talk to her whether he goes simple / fantasy/ cinematic/ new/ any indirect approach.

Basically, every woman has their own expectations of her imaginative world king of her dreams. When his approach makes her so reach or so special, she will feel positivity and she is ready to talk with him.

Even if he is not reached to her expectations also, she will enjoy his way of approach and his struggle to talk with her and also, she will see the sincerity of that person and mainly how much he dares himself if he not did wrong which is more important in anyone's life.

First Approach

"She will enjoy and observe every minute things which many of men will neglect. In this women see the nature of men and how he takes a initative towards life or any aspect."

She will only expect at this stage only a good behavior and also, she tries to test you in many ways which men can't guess that whether she is saying truth or testing because she can play multiple roles

more than Oscar actor in real life.

In the initial days of talking, she loves to hear your way of likes, what he does all times, future plans, what are expectations of future life partner.

Most importantly many men say to impress like you if I get, I be happy like that but she knows that its lie and he is tries to impress her or bluff her and mostly she feels like it was a lie inside of course it is a part of impressing her.

She in mean time she likes to talk about her life and also her personal family because it tries to make understanding her and her situations in daily time.

Many men will ignore that because many men like to talk about herself not about family. but people who are serious in love they only care about her feelings, situations and all.

Initial Talk Stage

She also like to listen his family and also in mean time many men don't disclose many things about his life also. he always thinks to impress her and also expect to love him again.

She will only think that he needs to be as himself not as bluffing.

She thinks and observe and remember each and everything whatever he says in mean time of talks whether it's true or false or he is tries to impress her.

> *"Many think she not have that mind to understand and also, he will try to bluff many times and also lie to her and say what all possibilities to make him pretend as good person in all men society."*

But that is the main mistake done by him.

4

Meeting

This point is very important to her because it reflects also the true character and intention of him about her and what is way of thinking.

Every woman wants to be special in one's life like her fathers after that friend after that loved one and also husband and finally kids.

She only expects a little bit of love and caring, If possible, some gifts.

She always wants to be as a normal daily meeting without making any extra addon colors or any unnatural of his behavior or any other unnecessary activities.

Meeting in a Public Place

She doesn't think all comes in a sudden

she thinks everything need to come with a little bit of time proportional way. If it happens all of a suddenly means then it is an indication of not correct person or not a correct time to do.

She will also see the way out of place what type of place you choose and how is it?

She also notices the things which type food you order and how you have it? in this time many men try to showcase that of the orders a stylish or costly food she will impress but as many say what we like we need to eat that only not as unlikely food.

> *"She will like to go out and like to time spend with you. She always wants to give importance both people's choice and come into open argument not to be as hiding or compromising things."*

5

Stage of Understanding

At this stage, she only checks and test you understanding levels of future, about her, about situations and about many problems.

She observes how you will take those situations or problems and how will solve with your understanding levels; in that she can say about her own life or friends' life or any other cinematic imaginations or any friends' suggestions also.

Understanding

It doesn't mean that she doubting you or any misunderstanding. She wants to know how much capable you and how much you understand her deeply inside her.

Many men in the time of talking with the women they try to impress and show a lot of imaginary and false stacks, in the understanding time those are also makes many changes. So be as how you are don't try to be some other which is not you.

"She wants exactly he needs to be very frankly and genuine way."

6

Love Him?

In this stage, she will think very seriously and very deeply about thinking of many things like his mindset, his approach, his understanding, his capability, his character, his attitude, his behavior, his good or bad, his life plans, his qualities everything gets into this place.

She also thinks at this stage how she or he can convince family and how it goes wrong or right way.

In this time she considers your talent, way of approach which she observed in the first approach towards her, talking is consdiered by her like how you talk with her, convincing is obviously some time we may wrong or late or something then how you take is looked into, skills etc. into consideration. This all comes with your true behaviour is shown otherwise the love is not love its a drama.

Love

She also thinks what if he stops loving him?

This is a very big question which any women or men think before saying or expressing their love towards their loved people. Because, they don't want to loose the love which was showing by their loveable person in their life.

She also thinks what if he got bored of her?

This question is something starts in middle or starting or end stage of relationship

She also thinks what if he not looking over her?

This is very big question thinking by mainly by men. That if she is not looking in the way of love then this friendship also not there!!!! But one thing everyone need to consider truth is " If you started love then it will never comes to Friendship Stage it always be in that Stage only"

She also thinks what if he sees other?
This comes with doubt or possesiveness feeling.

"Like this main thing when she ready to say love you too many questions need to get tick mark which can be happened by his original behavior only not by the blushing behavior."

7

Vulnerability

She also thinks what if she accepts his love and whether she can stay without him or not?

As many says women once start love they only expect return love only nothing more than that so, she completely addicted to the love, time spend, life of emotions, etc. with him. So she also thinks what if something happened wrong whether she can able to stay or not....

She also thinks whether he will back on her or not if she is in trouble?

Normally, the problems will come in many aspects when you are into a relationship or not. But when you are in a relationship the number of problems are more in many aspects like, Economical, Career, Life, Family, Friends, Society etc. These problems may errupt from her or his side. But she thinks if any problem is errupted by her knowing or unknowingly then what he will do? Whether he will back on me or leave me!!!!!

She also thinks how much value towards him about her?

"She also thinks How much serious about the relationship with her?"

Like this many things which may get mad or life taking chances happens or after marriage divorce changes will happened because of reason of failure of all above things.

Love in Mind

8 Opens Heart

"*Once she accepts then how he will take it?*"

How he will change?

whether he will be as same as how he will be? or any other different world of atmosphere will outburst

She always opens her heart very easily and with lots of hopes and happiness inside her.

She also scared about what if she started accepted and thought dreams of life with him but what if his originality will come out and her situation?

She will go into most turmoil stage. She will enter into many new stages of stress, pain, unfolded fear, fake smile, fake expressions, fake life, no dreams, no life, etc. everything in a glimpse it will flush her very deeply inside her.

Enter Caption

9

Commitment

She also starts thinking about what if she gives all herself about her life, dreams, secrets, and many more her imaginations shared to him by believing him.

She always wants to give her 200% of herself to him without being anything inside her any instance of time.

She always cares about him, his health, his food, his caring, his love, his value, even his economic conditions.

She will forget about her in mean time she only thinking about him and relationship with him.

She is scared of being commitment because what if once she commitment towards the relationship, then what happens if it ends up with no cards to play or no things of life are in her hands to be again as

How she is?

....

"She loses her confidence, her maturity, her morality, her ethics, her commitments, her love, her care, in fact she loses life of hope."

"She started live as machine with no emotions only anger, grief, pain, etc. will come."

10 Left In

In mean time of commitment her life will totally changes.

Before commitment she has her world of life with dreams, family, future and parents etc.

Once She commitment given towards him on thinking of a relationship with him.

Her world will change to only around one person is himself.

She will get scared what if it not up to the mark of things then her world will reverse as no one with her as how she has, they are with them, they are for her, all will leave her at that point of time which can't be reversable.

"She is very scared of being as no one."

11

Roller coaster

Mostly she will think and she scared more is what if he got his original out and says we have time to understand each other well and to let him again into herself.

She will think if he started understanding her on looking to her depth on that time where she has nothing left in her

She already lost herself on time of commitment and left in time.

She is really scared of not to be at this part of life.

She really scared of many emotional findings arise in her with a bunch of answers.

Enter Caption

12 Left Him

She was always wanted to be him in her life without leaving in a moment also.

Because she loved him truly, madly, deeply, heartfully and so enjoying.

But she scared of what if he left him as a person dropping in an island where no one staying or no one visit or no food is there?

She gets really mad on him not only him on whole men.

Because, once the heart breakup with full of poisoned true face the it can't be added with sugar which is useless.

In that time, she gets realizes that he is not hers anymore. He is being some others which can't make bring him back.

13 Alone

She always thinks very deeply and in future ways also.

If once she gets into one confusion state that whether he stay with her or not?

He would leave or not?

He understands her or not?

He committed to her or not?

He is himself or not?

He shows true face or not?

He making building on lies or not?

> *"Like many things makes him to push away from her life without any confusion."*

End

Finally,

> *"Suggestion for men - Be as who you are..."*

> *" Suggestion For Women - Be conscious will taking any decision."*

9 798885 697309

Printed by Libri Plureos GmbH in Hamburg, Germany